GEORGE'S GRAND ELEVATOR ADVENTURE

created & written by:

Mary Louise Franke

with illustrations by Evan Studwell

AuthorHouse™
1663 Liberty Drive
Bloomington, IN 47403
www.authorhouse.com
Phone: 833-262-8899

This book is printed on acid-free paper.

ISBN: 979-8-8230-3663-4 (sc)
ISBN: 979-8-8230-3664-1 (e)

Library of Congress Control Number: 2025913454

Print information available on the last page.

Published by AuthorHouse 10/29/2025

authorHOUSE®

GEORGE'S GRAND ELEVATOR ADVENTURE

WRITTEN BY: Mary Louise Franke
ILLUSTRATIONS BY: Evan Studwell

Dedication To: Alex
Little did I know that taking a walk with you and George would lead to "all of this" and more. Thank you for your endless love and unwavering support.

BASED ON TRUE EVENTS.

This is George, a five-year-old Doberman dog. He lives in the bustling city of Chicago with his mom and dad, on the sixth floor of a big apartment building. George loves cuddles, treats, basking in the sun, going on walks around the city, and playing with his best friend—his dad. Everyone in the neighborhood knows George!

One morning, George was resting before his family's move to a new apartment down the hall. Little did he know, an exciting adventure was waiting for him...

George was worried that the new apartment might not have a nice spot for sunbathing, so his dad took him to Chauncey's house to play.

George only stayed at Chauncey's for a little while. He was eager to get home and make sure the move went smoothly.

George's mom was loading a cart with trash to take down to the dumpster, and George decided to go with her.

When the elevator doors opened, Mom let George go in first.

Oops... the wheel of the cart got stuck in the elevator crack! Mom pulled the cart out to start over—but it was too late. The elevator doors were closing, and she couldn't stop them!

Mom pressed the button, but the doors didn't open. George was already on his way to another floor! Mom was frantic and called Dad for help.

George knew his mom would be upset. But his paws were itching, and his nose was twitching—he just had to go exploring!

Suddenly, door 531 opened, and out came a woman. She exclaimed to her husband, “Oh, honey! There’s the most handsome Doberman at our door! Millie would love for him to come say hi!”

The woman invited George in to meet Millie. The man liked George too, and he built a warm fire for George and Millie.

Then the woman brought out homemade doggie cookies.

After the yummy cookies and the cozy fire, George decided he’d better look for his parents. He knew they must be worried about him.

George trotted back toward the elevator—and just then, it happened to open! It was empty, so he hopped right in...

When George arrived on the fourth floor, he heard children's voices.

George loved children! He wagged his tail and strutted down the hallway to see what all the buzz was about...

401

A little boy peeked out and shouted,
“Julian! Vera! Look! There’s a big dog at the door!”

Julian laughed and said,
“Griffin, nice try—but you’re not fooling me!”

Before he knew it, George was in the living room, playing with the three kids. They climbed all over him, giggling and laughing until their cheeks ached from smiling.

At last, when they were worn out from all the fun, the children curled up on George and drifted off to sleep.

When George awoke, he remembered he should be looking for his parents. He made sure each child was sound asleep... then quietly slipped away.

When the elevator doors opened, George hopped on. The elevator was empty… but someone had pressed a button, and it started moving!

When the doors opened on the third floor, George saw an elderly man struggling to carry a heavy shopping bag. The bag slipped from the man's hands and fell to the floor.

Quick as a flash, George grabbed the bag by the handles in his mouth and helped the man carry it into unit 331.

As he opened the door, George walked right into unit 331. The elderly man joined his three friends at the poker table for their weekly game.

The men welcomed George with open arms. One of them chuckled, “Looks like we’ve got ourselves a fifth player...”

As the men played, George listened as they swapped stories and shared memories.

But soon, George began to miss his own family. After receiving his last head pats, he wagged his tail and started on his way again...

Down and away went George, taking the elevator to the second floor. There, a delicious smell tickled his nose—something he especially loved. Could it be bacon?

He followed his nose to 227. Gently, he pawed at the door...

A little pup peeked out through the puppy entrance and helped George squeeze inside!

George spotted the bacon in a bowl. Regina could tell he wanted some, so she ate half and kindly gave the rest to George.

George and Regina began playing together, but suddenly, George heard a man from the next room yell, “Hey, Regina! What are you doing in there?”

Alarmed, George gave Regina a sweet goodbye and squeezed out the puppy door.

He was smitten by Regina, but he really wanted to find his mom and dad—so back to the elevator he went.

George got back on the elevator and rode down to the first floor. When the doors opened, he saw the lobby.

He could smell his mom... and just as he was about to turn the corner, he saw his dad's tall shadow and ran toward the front desk.

The doorman spotted George and called out, "It's George!"

George's parents were overjoyed to see him!

They all hugged tightly and took one last ride on the elevator for the day. By the time they reached their new apartment, the sun was setting...

George ran out onto the balcony and hopped up into his chair. Mom said, “George, I hope you weren’t too scared today! We were so worried…”

George looked up with his big puppy eyes and thought, “Scared? I just had the best day ever! But I’m happy to be home… I hope Dad takes me to the park tomorrow so I can run and play with Karl and Gary…”

Dad smiled and said, “We’re glad you’re home, George. Tomorrow we’ll go to the park and meet up with your dog buddies…”

As the night sky settled in, George and his family were grateful to be together.

George was ready for a good night’s rest. He knew he would be up and out on the balcony again as soon as the sunlight streamed through his window…

THE END

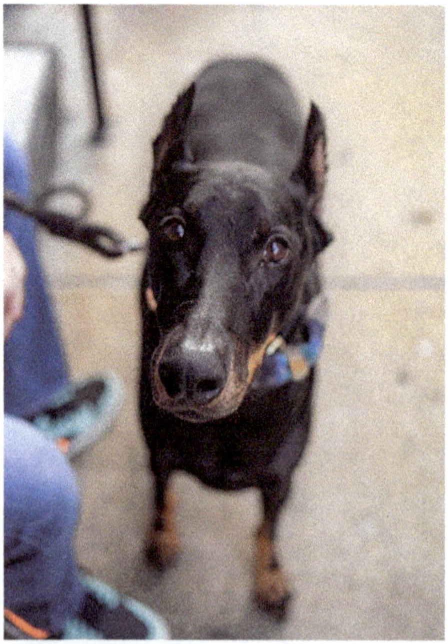

About the Author

Mary lives in Chicago, Illinois, with George and her fiancé, Alex. She is the Director of Youth Education at a professional acting school, where she also teaches acting classes for children of all ages. A graduate of Loyola University Chicago with a degree in acting, Mary began performing professionally soon after graduation and continues to pursue her passion today.

This is her first book, and she looks forward to sharing more stories from George's adventures. When she isn't teaching, writing, or acting, Mary loves exploring the beautiful city of Chicago with George and Alex.

www.ingramcontent.com/pod-product-compliance
Lightning Source LLC
Chambersburg PA
CBHW042220011225
36191CB00058B/2273
* 9 7 9 8 8 2 3 0 3 6 6 3 4 *